YOU RAISE ME UP

A NOVELLA BY

ALANA TERRY

ONE

My name is Lucy Jean, but I insist on being called Grandma Lucy.

I should warn you starting out that my mind isn't quite as sharp as it once was. I hope that's all right with you. What I'm saying is that I've got a story to tell you, except I can't always be sure that I'm getting things down exactly the same way as they really happened. Comes from getting older, I suppose.

I've lived a long life on God's beautiful earth, and I'm tremendously thankful to say that the good Lord has sustained me for all these years, and I have no doubt he'll continue to do so until the day he calls me heavenward.

I make my home in Washington. We've got a little farm in a small town named Orchard Grove. Maybe you've heard of it. Kind people. Small community. My niece and I raise goats there. Well, Connie tends the goats, but I declare she's getting up there in years too and really needs to hire help.

If my own niece is a senior citizen, I wonder what that says about me and my age!

We do serve a wonderful Lord, don't we? He's so good to us in all his ways. I was just telling my grandson about it the other day. Let him know that it's high time he realizes all the things he's going through in life are God's way of getting his attention. That's the problem with young people. When something bad happens or things don't go their way, they automatically assume God's out to get them.

If they even believe in God at all, I should add.

Ian doesn't. Not yet. But he will. I know it's going to happen.

He's had a sad life, my grandson. Mother killed by a drunk driver, and him so little. He and his sister both. Alayna's doing well these days. Married to a pastor so far out in the country in Alaska those poor folks are hauling their own water. But they're doing God's work, Alayna and her little family.

Ian's the one I worry about most. He's got such a compassionate streak, my grandson does. Always talking about this injustice or that oppressed people group. And I love him for it, believe me. Some Christians stick up their noses at that type of thing, which I just consider hogwash. All you've got to do is flip open to any passage in the Old Testament, and you'll see that God is a warrior for justice. Yes, he is.

Well, my grandson makes his living traveling the world. He's a reporter, by the way, in case I hadn't mentioned that earlier. He's building a pretty big name for himself, too. Recently helped make a full documentary about that terrible tragedy in Detroit. You've heard of it by now, I'm sure. After what happened on Flight 219, everybody in the world's heard about it, no doubt.

Short story is there's a school for little kids in Detroit that never should have been built. You'd have to ask my grandson to give you all the details because as a journalist he's better with the facts. But kids were getting sick. Parents were worried about long-term damage just because the particular spot where this school was built used to be a pharmacy factory, making all those pills, and that was before there were better safety regulations, so they didn't handle their waste properly at all.

I feel so sorry for those poor kids and sorry for their parents too. But that certainly doesn't excuse what General and his batch of criminals did to my flight when I was only trying to get home last December.

I'd gone to see Ian, the grandson I was just telling you about. He travels all over the world, like I mentioned, and was about to take off on another trip. He's been working on a documentary about North Korean refugees, and I told him the day he started it several years ago I had a bad feeling about that place. The North Korean government really doesn't take kindly to Americans poking around in their business, if you know what I mean, and I worry for my grandson, which may surprise you, seeing as how I've developed something of a reputation as a prayer warrior. Truth be told, I'm a worry-wart, and that's the perfect truth, especially when it comes to my grandchildren. It'd be different if Ian was saved already, but he hasn't accepted Christ as his personal Lord and Savior. Not yet. So I told him, "Ian, it's one thing if you go to North Korea and get yourself captured there after I'm perfectly convinced that your soul's made its peace with God. It's totally different if you're still walking in rebellion to him. I'm worried for you."

And he always says the same thing to me. That he's not going into North Korea, he's just interviewing refugees who've made it out to China. He promises me he'll be safe, but I'm not so sure. Call it a premonition if you will. I just don't like him going over there all by himself.

You'd think with him spending so much time in Asia, I'd be thrilled. That's where I grew up, actually. My parents were missionaries in Shanghai. In fact, my father owned and operated one of China's first bookstores and printing companies for Bibles and Christian literature. You can't do that type of thing now, not unless you have special government permission, but back then things were a little different.

Of course, the political climate at the time was pretty unstable, but we managed.

Even saw ourselves through the bombings of Shanghai, but that's a story for another day.

I was telling you about Ian, wasn't I? That's where I was. So, my grandson lives out near Boston, even though, like I told you earlier, he's traveling all the time. I really do pray that one day God sends him a nice young woman to help ease that restless burden in his soul. I sure would love to see that boy settled down before the good Lord calls me home to glory.

Anyway, I was on Flight 219 because I'd been out East to visit my grandson. See him off before another one of his trips around the world. I wanted him to hear the gospel one last time as well, so we went out to dinner, and I spelled it out to him plainly. He's a sinner, just like we all are, and unless he repents and ask God to forgive him, he'll remain lost.

Ian's a smart boy. Graduated from Harvard, even. But he doesn't like to be told that he's wrong. Thank the good Lord, we have a good relationship, and he knows I'm only telling him these things because I love him so much.

What I did was plant some seeds. It's up

to God now to water them and make them grow.

That's why I pray for Ian as hard as I do. For Ian and all my other grandkids and great-grandkids who aren't walking with the Lord. Not yet. I pray that God would open their eyes to the glorious truths of his Word, that he'd send them conviction when they need it, that he'd make them so unmistakably aware of his love for them and his presence in their lives.

It's one thing to know about God. It's quite another thing to know him personally.

I went decades not understanding the difference, squandered years of my life before the good Lord showed me some sense. But that's a story for another day.

TWO

I wasn't supposed to be on that particular flight, not originally.

I'd visited my grandson, I'd told him what I flew out there to say, and then it was time to leave Ian's soul in God's hands and fly myself home. Connie doesn't like me traveling alone. Says I'm too old for that. I suppose one day I might need to slow down, but I don't think that day's here.

Not yet.

There were snowstorms in the Midwest. Lots of flights were getting cancelled or delayed. If I'm remembering correctly, originally I was meant to fly from Boston to Chicago, and from Chicago on home. I was looking forward to it too because last year when I was flying through Chicago, I met a woman who served me tea at a little restaurant, and she looked so sad, and I asked her what was wrong, and she told me a tragic story about how the foster father she loved like her daddy had just gotten shot, and more than anything she wanted to be there to spend her Christmas with him, except she didn't have any money and was desperately worried about her father.

Well, I prayed with her, and I ended up sharing the gospel with her too. I figure if God's granted me the chance to travel and hasn't decided to take me home yet, that's just because there's more people here on this earth like that worried waitress he wants me to witness to.

Fine by me. I know my marching orders.

Anyway, I gave that young woman my phone number, and she promised to be in touch, but I haven't heard from her since. I don't know if her father survived his injuries, if she made it to be with her family that Christmas or not. More than anything, I want to know if she took anything that I said to her that day to heart. She told me she grew up in a Christian foster home. Her father was actually a pastor out East.

But you can have a saint for a parent and still not be saved. Just look at me. My parents were missionaries during some of the most dangerous periods in China's history. And even then I didn't come to know the Lord personally until well into my adulthood.

But that's a story for another day.

Well, I'd been looking forward to reconnecting with that waitress in Chicago. Then my flight got cancelled, and the airlines decided to fly me out to Detroit instead to catch my next plane from there. Well I told God that was fine with me. I figured the Almighty had that nice young waitress taken care of, and instead there must be somebody in Detroit I was meant to minister to. Either that or maybe somebody on the airplane.

I could tell even while I was waiting for my flight that the Lord was working mightily behind the scenes. Some days I travel and use the waiting periods to pray and think about all the blessings God's poured out on me during my long life on his beautiful earth. Other times, he just seems to send one person after another my way, people I can share the gospel with or give a little word of encouragement to.

That's what happened in the airport while I was waiting for Flight 219.

First it was a young mother traveling alone with her little boy. He was a real sweetie too. Perfect manners. Absolute gentleman.

Turns out they were headed to Detroit, but the flight they were on was cancelled, and this little tyke was so sad he wasn't going to be able to see his grandma for Christmas. Well, the good news was I'd been at my gate by then for a little while and knew they were calling standbys, so I told them they should see about getting on my plane.

I had a real heart to pray for that young woman. She struck me as anxious. Sad. When her son said they were visiting their grandma, I could tell his mom wasn't nearly as excited as he was.

And so I prayed for her.

Prayed that God would be working behind the scenes to restore her relationships. To bless her little boy. To show them both just how incredibly he loves them and wants what's best in their lives.

I still pray for her, by the way. I don't know her name, but I've added her and that darling little boy of hers to my prayer list.

When I first started praying for them each afternoon from my prayer room, I got such a heavy sense of sadness, but now my prayers feel lighter. I hope that means this young mother has finally found some peace. When I talk to Jesus about that little boy, my heart's just filled with joy. I'm convinced he's going to grow up to change the world for Christ. I just know it. Sometimes I get a sense about these things. And I might be wrong sometimes, but in this case I have no doubts.

Well, I kept on waiting for my flight, kept on running into other passengers. And it's interesting. It really is when you sit back and realize just how intertwined our lives all are. It's like a novel, where each of the characters comes in and out of the story, and you realize there's somebody at work behind the scenes. There just has to be. These things don't happen by chance.

But I suppose you didn't come here to chat with me about the people I met and prayed with before we boarded Flight 219, did you? It's interesting though, isn't it? How we're in a spiritual war each and every day. And yet it's things that happen in this temporal world that make the news. A plane getting hijacked. A young girl being kidnapped.

That's the only danger most people see. They have no idea about the spiritual battle raging on around us each and every day. I suppose the devil likes to keep us blind like that. If we spend our whole lives scared of terrorists and kidnappers and murderers, we almost forget that the real battle is for our souls.

Flight 219 was a war zone, both in the physical and spiritual senses. God gifted me a premonition of the attack before it started. I was at the gate praying with another passenger when he gave me the vision. Maybe you want to know why I didn't sound the alarm, let somebody know. Well it doesn't quite work like that. See, I didn't know if God was giving me a picture of my own flight or someone else's. I didn't know if the danger was going to happen today or five years from now.

All I saw was a plane going down in smoke. I could hear the screams of the passengers. And there I was in the back of the cabin, my hands outstretched just like Moses while the Israelites fought in the valley below him, and I was praying for God to uphold that plane.

That's what I saw.

It could have meant almost anything.

It could have meant that God was showing me what he was protecting me from.

It could have meant that God was prompting me to pray for my grandson and his flight to China.

It could have meant that I'm an old, old woman with an active imagination, and sometimes when I let my mind wander during my prayers, I see pictures that don't mean a single thing.

Like that time God gave me a dream about a goat in labor, and I was so sure it meant our little doe was in trouble, and I made Connie get out of bed and her husband too, and we all went to check, and everything was fine.

But that's a story for another day.

At the airport, when I was praying with another passenger before we were supposed to board, I saw an image of fire and smoke and a cabin full of terrified passengers.

It wasn't until that man knocked out the air marshal that I realized exactly what my vision meant.

And by then, it was too late.

THREE

I'VE BEEN in scary situations before. You don't get to be my age without going through your fair share of fear and trauma. That's the way life works, isn't it?

I'm certainly not afraid to die. I figure that statistically speaking, it's going to happen soon. And since I'm not really keen on the idea of weeks or months in a hospital bed, drifting in and out of consciousness, it's not that frightening to picture myself getting shot in the head.

People who know me, people who've read about that flight ask me about it quite a lot. Did I know what was going to happen when I stood up to General? Did I know his gun was going to misfire?

No, I didn't.

But that doesn't make me a hero. Not in the least.

I'm getting ahead of myself, though. I suppose if I'm going to tell this story, I should try to stick to things in the order they happened. That's harder to do than it sounds, you know. Sometimes I wonder how people like Ian manage who make their living from writing words all day.

On the airplane, I was seated toward the back. There was a family who got on then got off again before they closed the doors. I think it was God giving the mother a feeling, warning her that something was about to go terribly wrong.

I've added that family to my prayer list as well. They looked so nice, all dressed up for their flight. I remember when that was the thing to do. You'd never travel anywhere without putting on your Sunday best. Now, people show up at the airport in sweats or flannels. Look like they're still in their pajamas. I suppose if that's how they feel the most comfortable, that's fine with me, but it's one thing that made this family stand out to me all the more.

The mother wore a long denim skirt. So

did her daughters. The father was young but had a long beard. Made me wonder if the man had ever seen a razor in his life. They were quiet. Sweet. But there was something in the mother's eyes that caught my attention. A fear she was trying to hide.

I've been praying for her quite a bit these days. I'm afraid I can't recall just how many kids she had and how many of them were boys and how many were girls, so I focus on praying for her. She's the one I remember most.

And in my prayers, I ask God to ease that fear she's been carrying around for so long. He sure is an amazing Lord, isn't he? Big enough to bear our burdens, even the ones that feel like they're going to drown us in despair.

I think about that young mother, and I think about Psalm 91. Are you familiar with that one? It's such a beautiful blessing to pray over anyone who's frightened.

Whoever dwells in the shelter of the Most High will rest in the shadow of the Almighty. I will say of the Lord, "He is my refuge and my fortress, my God, in whom I trust."

Such a beautiful promise, isn't it? And how encouraging to picture ourselves resting in the shadow of the Almighty. So many times we think of shadows as places of fear and uncertainty, of darkness. Like the shadow of death.

Except this verse is different. It's talking about the shadow of the Almighty and the rest we find ourselves in when we're safe within his protective care.

Surely he will save you from the fowler's snare and from the deadly pestilence.

God brought this verse to mind a few decades ago when I was going to return to China on a missionary trip. I don't live there anymore, obviously, but I've never forgotten my second home where I grew up. I've lost track of how many times I've returned there since I've given my life entirely over to Christ. Maybe six or seven? I go carrying Scripture. They call me a Bible donkey. The idea of it sure makes me laugh. Well I was all set to go on one of my Bible smuggling trips when the bird flu epidemic broke out. Do you remember that?

My family didn't want me traveling to Asia. Said it was too dangerous. So I just reminded them of Psalm 91. Told them that God promised to save me from the fowler's snare and from the deadly pestilence. If that isn't a reference to divine protection from bird flu, then my name isn't Lucy Jean.

I used to have that entire chapter memorized, all of Psalm 91, I mean. Now, it's harder to recall the verses all at once, but I trust that God will bring the right ones to mind when I need them most.

I'm afraid I've been rambling so much I forgot what I'd started telling you about in the first place.

But when I'm rocking in my prayer chair, those are the verses that come to mind when I pray for the young mother who God used to get her family off that plane.

To safety.

FOUR

I DON'T KEEP up with the news all that much. I figure that if there's something happening in the world God wants me to pray for, he's going to let me know about it whether or not I pick up a paper. I guess lots of people have written about me in articles and things like that. Say I saved the whole plane for what I did, standing between the gunman and his victim.

Well, that's not how I see it, and if you want to know the full truth, I think most of those stories are blowing things out of proportion. General was holding a gun, about to shoot a young girl barely past her teens. I told him if he wanted to kill someone that badly, it may as well be me. I've already explained to you before my philosophy on death. If it's a bang from a bullet and then I'm in heaven, don't you think that sounds more bearable than languishing for years in a nursing home?

Now, if I were younger, if I still had kids to look after for example, we wouldn't be having this discussion at all. But the death of an old lady who's already raised her kids and grandkids and has lived to see multiple great-grands is far less distressing than the death of a young girl who's not even lived a quarter of her life yet. Even an evolutionist who doesn't believe an ounce of Scripture would agree with me on that one.

The young woman I allegedly saved is named Willow. I know that because I was chatting for a while with her roommate on the plane. Kennedy and Willow. Two college girls traveling home to visit Alaska.

They weren't what you'd expect at first in best friends. Kennedy was quiet and studious. We got to talking, and I learned that she grew up on the mission field in China as well. I don't believe in coincidences, but this was most certainly a wink from the Almighty if I've ever experienced one.

She was a sweet girl, that Kennedy. A

little bit timid, still unaware of the amazing power of the Holy Spirit residing in her. But she's learning. I get the sense when I pray for her that God has amazing and dramatic plans for Kennedy's life. The kind of story you'd like to see made into a movie or listen to as one of those old-fashioned radio dramas.

I also get the sense that Flight 219 wasn't the last time I'll be crossing paths with this sweet, young daughter of God. But maybe that's just the wishful thinking of an old woman like me.

Well, inasmuch as Kennedy was quiet and sweet and kind, her best friend Willow was quite the opposite. Not in a bad way, mind you. It wasn't like she was brash or rude. Just louder. More vibrant. The first thing you'd notice about Willow if you met her was her hair. Dyed bright blue. Don't ask me why someone would take such gorgeous locks and style them that way. I guess that's just what some young people like to do these days. I'll never understand it, but that doesn't mean I should judge.

Willow was sitting with a young man on the flight, which gave me the chance to get to know Kennedy more. And we talked about it. How Willow isn't a believer. Not yet, I should say. How Kennedy wanted to share the gospel with her friend but still hadn't figured out how.

I sensed a lot of fear in Kennedy. She's another one that when I pray for her, Psalm 91 comes to mind. *If you say, "The Lord is my refuge," and you make the Most High your dwelling, no harm will overtake you, no disaster will come near your tent. For he will command his angels concerning you to guard you in all your ways; they will lift you up in their hands, so that you will not strike your foot against a stone.*

I guess it's a meaningful verse when you're talking about a stranger you meet on a hijacked flight.

For he will command his angels concerning you to guard you in all your ways. I can't say for sure that I've met a real angel before, but I have my suspicions. Like that time when I was a kid and Shanghai was getting bombed and my mother and I were trying to reach home. There was a man who claimed to be a French diplomat who just showed up to our aid, but that's a story for another day.

I absolutely believe that angels are surrounding us, protecting us from harm. And yet there are so many believers just like

Kennedy who still feel scared of sharing the gospel.

My prayer for her is that God will fill her up with incredible boldness, that the fear of man will no longer have a hold on her, and that she'll finally learn how to tap into that amazing power she has as an anointed child of God.

I'm trying to think if there was anything else to tell you about what happened before the flight got taken over. I'm sure I talked to other passengers, but like I said, I'm afraid I don't recall details quite as clearly as I used to. There was a young woman in first class I prayed with while I was waiting to use the bathrooms. I would have added her to my prayer list as well, but I'm embarrassed to admit I can't recall what it was we prayed about or why God prompted me to stop and talk with her in the first place.

I'm sure at this point you want to hear all about the hijacking itself, but I'm afraid I have bad news for you there, too.

I slept right through it.

I'm telling you the gospel truth. After I talked with Kennedy a while and we prayed for her friend Willow's salvation, I went to use the bathroom and stopped and prayed with someone else (although like I said, I can't seem to remember who). Then I headed to the back of the plane and took a little nap. When I woke up, a man was waving a gun at Willow, the young woman I'd been praying for just an hour or so earlier.

So that's when I stood up and did what any other believer in my situation would do.

FIVE

When the family came over for dinner a few weeks ago, everyone wanted to hear that part of the story.

What I was feeling. Wasn't I scared. Did I have any idea the gun wouldn't go off. How did I ever get to be so brave.

Really, the answer to all those questions is simple.

I knew Willow wasn't saved, which meant that I couldn't stand by and watch her die. Not while I had the chance to do something to help her.

The news articles and blog posts tell me I preached for five or ten minutes with the hijacker's gun pointed at my head. I'm afraid I don't remember that part either, so I can't give you many details about what I said.

But I know people have read about me in the news. At one point there was even speculation that I might be an angel because apparently nobody could find me when the airport security folks were conducting their interviews after we landed. There's actually a really good reason for that.

Nobody told me I needed to stick around, and I wasn't injured at all, so I decided that what I really needed was a good night's rest. I got off the plane and found myself a quiet gate in the airport, and I napped until the next morning. Then I woke myself up and talked with a sweet young man serving coffee at a little donut shop whose wife is expecting their very first baby, a tiny boy with Down's syndrome, but that's a story for another day.

I don't like the fact that my actions on Flight 219 have been turned into something spectacular. It wasn't that at all. But I do know people want to hear my side of the story, and since I can't remember at all what I said or felt while I was trying to talk the gunman down, let me tell you about my prayers for him since then.

I don't believe in praying for the dead. That's just superstitious mumbo-jumbo. General died in the fire. I know some people are upset he won't face the American justice system, but I'm certain that God's justice is quite a bit more powerful and to be feared.

So I don't bother praying for General, not because I don't care about him or the state of his soul when he passed, but because he's already gone. He had his chance on earth to get right with God. And who knows? Maybe he did right before he drew his last breath. We won't know about that until we reach heaven.

But I do pray for General's kids. They're so young still. It's not their fault their father took over an airplane and murdered those innocent people. Unfortunately, I worry that General's children will blame themselves since after all it was their school General was so upset about.

I guess if anything good has come from this, it's that the Detroit school district has closed down Brown Elementary. The students enrolled there are currently being taught in trailers at nearby schools, but plans are underway for a new building, funded mostly by private donations.

I'm thankful for that much at least. But it's such a shame the way it all came about, isn't it?

So I've added General's children to my daily prayer list. I pray that God would give them maturity beyond their years to see and understand that their father loved them, but he needed help. Like I said, I don't pay much attention to news reports, but there've been quite a bit of rumblings about General's mental health. Who knows? With the right doctors and a lot of prayer, maybe he could have run for mayor of Detroit or gotten himself elected superintendent himself and brought about change for his children in a much more positive way.

It's too late for anything like that to happen now, though.

And so I pray. Day in, day out. When I can't sleep, I make my way down to my prayer room. Sit in my rocking chair, talking to God.

I talk to him about the passengers I met on that flight. The mother in the long skirt who took her children off the plane. The mom traveling with that sweet little boy. That studious college student Kennedy and her blue-haired best friend.

I pray for them all.

I pray for God to cover over the fear and the trauma they endured on that flight.

I pray for the Almighty to wash over them with his peace that surpasses all understanding.

I read Psalm 91 and I pray the verses over them. Pray that God would protect them, that he would be with them in trouble, that he will deliver them and show them his salvation.

And I pray for you too, my sweet and faithful reader. I pray that your heart and soul today would be filled with the riches and fulness of God's grace. I pray that he would open the eyes of your heart so that you might grasp and understand how wide and how long and how high and how deep is his amazing love for you.

I pray that he will sustain you through sadness and sickness and trials, and that when you reach the last chapter of your life on God's beautiful earth, you'll be able to say with confidence along with the Apostle Paul, "I have fought the good fight, I have finished the race, I have kept the faith."

That is my prayer for you, and that's

what I ask God on your behalf each and every time I talk with him.

But that's a story for another day.

FROM ALANA: Thanks so much for joining me on this journey.

The idea for the Turbulent Skies Christian Thriller novellas came to me over three years ago, when I was flying to California to visit my grandparents.

I was people-watching on the plane (as authors tend to do), trying to come up with backstories for each of the passengers. It was both awe-inspiring and a little overwhelming to realize that God knew every single person on that plane (and their stories) so intimately.

I tucked the idea for a thriller series set on a hijacked airplane in the back of my head and focused on other novels.

Grandma Lucy was first introduced in the book *Turbulence*, which is book 5 in the Kennedy Stern Christian suspense series, my most popular collection of novels to date. This book gives the story of Flight 219 from

Kennedy's perspective as she's traveling to Alaska with her best friend Willow.

Grandma Lucy's character is based in large part on my own grandmother, who was raised as a missionary kid in Shanghai and who returned to China multiple times to smuggle Bibles. My grandmother died the week before I started writing *Turbulence*. I thought that basing a character on this prayer warrior would be a neat way to commemorate her, and I know if she were still alive, she'd get a kick out of reading about herself in my books.

I'm so thankful for the legacy of prayer and evangelism and missions my Grandma not only lived but passed down the generations, and I know my life has been irrevocably blessed by all her prayers for me and my family. The world lost a tremendous prayer warrior the day my grandma died, which is one reason why it's always so special for me whenever I get the chance to write about her in some of my novels.

Grandma Lucy also plays a large part in the Orchard Grove books. These are different than my typical Christian suspense novels and fall more into the women's fiction category. In the Orchard Grove series, three young women attend a church service where Grandma Lucy offers the closing prayer. Each one of these women is impacted by her words in a significant yet different way.

If you haven't read the Kennedy Stern Christian suspense series yet, where Grandma Lucy is first introduced and where Kennedy and her roommate Willow experience dangerous encounters that test their faith and keep readers turning pages WAY past their bedtime, grab the first three novels in the Kennedy Stern series on sale now.

Dive into the Kennedy Stern series today! ... Or keep reading for a sneak peek from *Turbulence*, the Kennedy Stern novel where Kennedy and Willow first meet Grandma Lucy on Flight 219.

TURBULENCE

T minus 1 hour 43 minutes

"Gladys Aylward? What a remarkable woman."

Kennedy was startled by the interruption to her reading.

A white-haired woman with thin-rimmed spectacles and a blouse that might have been ordered from a 1970s Sears catalog smiled at her. "I'm sorry, the restroom up front was occupied, so I came back here and couldn't help but notice your book. Are you enjoying the story?"

Kennedy didn't feel up to chatting, but since the back lavatory was occupied as well, she didn't think she had much choice. "Yeah. It's pretty interesting."

"They made a movie about her life. Did you know that?"

Kennedy shook her head.

"Well, it's quite an old one. The actress who starred in it — oh, I wish I could remember her name just now, but that's what happens when your brain gets as old as mine. Anyway, the story goes this woman became a Christian after playing the role. I assume then that you're a born-again believer?"

That phrase always struck Kennedy as strange. A *born-again believer*, as if there were any other kind. "Yeah. I am." No use getting into a theological debate on an airplane with an eighty-year-old grandmother.

A flight attendant tapped the woman on the shoulder. "Excuse me, can I squeeze past you, please?"

The old lady sat down in the Mennonite mother's empty spot and glanced at the bathroom. "Looks like I might be here a while." She smiled warmly. "My name is Lucy Jean, but I insist on being called Grandma Lucy."

"I'm Kennedy," she replied automatically, wondering how long the bathroom occupant would take.

"Kennedy. What a lovely name. You know, I still wish my parents had come up with something more creative than Lucy Jean. You don't get much plainer than that."

Kennedy was about to protest that it was an attractive name when Grandma Lucy asked, "Are you going to Detroit today?"

"No, I'm on my way to Seattle and then Anchorage to spend Christmas with my friend's family."

"How lovely. I have a granddaughter in Alaska."

"Is that where you're going?" Kennedy asked.

"No, I'm getting off in Seattle. Going home to Washington. I was just in Boston to see off my grandson. He's on his way to ..." She stopped herself to finger Kennedy's necklace from across the aisle. "What in the world is this? It looks New Age."

All Kennedy wanted to do was get back to her reading, but she gave her best impression of a smile. "It's an air purifier. You wear it around your neck, and it filters out germs and dust. My roommate got them for us for the flight." She nodded toward Willow, who was watching some violent movie on her portable screen.

Grandma Lucy frowned at the gruesome image. "And your roommate?" she asked. "Is she born-again, too?"

Kennedy was spared the chore of stammering an awkward reply when the math teacher Willow had been flirting with came up to their row.

"Bathroom full?" he asked.

Willow plucked out her earbuds and offered her most winsome grin. "Hey, Ray. I was hoping we'd bump into each other during the flight."

Kennedy unbuckled her safety belt. "It looks like there's a line, so why don't you take my seat and I'll come over here." She stepped across the aisle and sat in the window seat beside Grandma Lucy. Her contacts were getting dry anyway, so now was probably as good a time as any to take a break from reading.

Grandma Lucy took Kennedy's hand in hers. Her skin was surprisingly soft for someone with so many wrinkles. "That was sweet of you, dear. Now let me take a look at you." She stared for several seconds before she gave her hand a squeeze. "You don't have to tell me. Let me guess. You're studying to be a missionary, aren't you?"

Kennedy slipped her hand away, surprised at how warm it felt. "A doctor, actually."

Grandma Lucy nodded, as if she had known that all along. "Medical missions, then?"

Kennedy didn't know what to say. Did Grandma Lucy's version of a *born-again believer* require some sort of ministry focus to prove your devotion?

"I'm not sure. I'm still doing my undergrad studies, so I guess I have plenty of time to figure that out." She let out an uncomfortable laugh.

Grandma Lucy chuckled too, tentatively as if she weren't sure what was so funny. "It's just that when I first looked at you, something in my spirit said *missionary*. I'm sure that's what I heard." She frowned and looked around her, as if her train of thought had derailed and she had to visibly track it down.

Kennedy had an unsettled feeling in the base of her spine. Why did it seem as though every other Christian on this flight was getting direct messages from the Lord except for her? Had God ever spoken to her that way before? Or maybe he had tried, and Kennedy just didn't know what to listen for.

"You're sure you're not a missionary?" Grandma Lucy pressed.

"No, but my parents are."

Grandma Lucy's face lit up before Kennedy could continue. "That's what it was. I knew you had a missions call on your life the moment I saw you with that book. My family was good friends with Gladys, you know. She came to visit us on more than one occasion when we lived in Shanghai."

"Really?" Kennedy's interest was piqued, and since Willow was busy laughing with her new travel partner, Kennedy figured she may as well try to enjoy her conversation.

"My parents were missionaries in China. I was born over there, in fact, and my father had a little Christian store he ran for decades before the Communists shut it down. When war broke out with Japan, we ran into Gladys on more than one occasion. She was taking care of so many kids!"

Lost in thought, Grandma Lucy continued to speak of her time in Shanghai during the Sino-Japanese War. Stories of bombings, narrow escapes from death, heroic ventures her father undertook to help the injured, the selfless sacrifices her mother made to assist the war orphans.

"Of course, she never took in as many as Gladys," Grandma Lucy remarked with a smile that lit up her whole face and pushed her spectacles up on her cheeks. "But she did what God called her to, which is all he expects from each one of us, isn't it?"

Kennedy nodded, even though her mind was still back in war-torn Shanghai where Grandma Lucy had recounted stories of fires and destruction as readily as if she were talking about Sunday picnics in Central Park.

"And what about you?" she finally asked. "You say you're in medical school?"

"Pre-med," Kennedy corrected and spent the next few minutes answering questions about life as an undergrad student at Harvard.

"And are you part of a good church body over there?"

"Yeah." Kennedy didn't admit that she only made it to St. Margaret's once or twice a month, fearing it might make Grandma Lucy rethink Kennedy's previous claim of being a true *born-again* believer.

"That's good." Grandma Lucy nodded sagely. "I ask because that grandson of mine I just visited, he graduated from Harvard a few years ago, and it filled him with so many idolatrous, liberal views of God and religion and the world." She sighed. "He's a great boy, don't get me wrong. Has a heart bigger than most Christians who fill the churches across this country. Gets worked up over injustice and actually does something about it. Just to give you an example, before he left for work in Asia, he was in Detroit of all places, interviewing parents about this issue they're having in the education system there. The schools, they're falling apart. Not just the system, I mean the actual buildings are falling apart. One school's pipes were so bad, they were leaking lead into the drinking fountains. Had been going on for years before anyone fixed it. Just terrible. And then this whole big mess over the Brown Elementary School. You heard about that whole controversy, I'm sure."

"Actually, no." Kennedy tried not to sound embarrassed at the confession. She'd been so busy with her studies that if her dad didn't send her a link from one of his conservative news sites or Pastor Carl didn't say anything about it from the pulpit, she'd never hear about a particular current event. Especially not one from as far away as Detroit.

Grandma Lucy shook her head. "Terrible thing. I don't have all the facts. You'd have to talk to Ian about that. But it has something to do with them closing down one elementary school and merging it with another. Well, that was the plan. But the school they needed to shut down was mostly minorities, and the one they were going to merge with was more upper-class, and those parents got themselves all worked up. Made such a stink that the school district decided to build a new school for the poor kids instead, except the site they were planning to build on was in a bad part of town. I'm not talking crime. That's bad just about everywhere in Detroit from what I hear.

"But where they planned the new building, the land itself was no good. All kind of contaminants in the soil, toxic waste from chemical factories. Except the parents of these students, they weren't like the upper-class folks. They're working families, lots of single parents who are at their jobs during the day and can't attend meetings and forums. Even the ones who have time, a lot of them don't speak English well and they're too intimidated to stand up for themselves. So my grandson, he went and documented everything, got some statements from the families and a few other community members to show just how bad things had gotten.

"He sold it to one of the major networks, had it all lined up to air on national television, but then that night some big breaking story took its spot. Something about a murdered politician if I remember right, and that hogged the news for the next week or two until it was past back-to-school season and his network contact said nobody wanted to think about the education system anymore.

"He was pretty upset, obviously, not because of the money or anything, but because he believed in what these parents were going through. Really felt for them, I mean. He told me what he hated most was seeing how the school district gave in to intimidation when it came from the upper-class folks. The rich ones had the clout they needed to make the right kind of noise, but these minority families — the ones whose kids are going to suffer most in this new school they're building — they don't get a say at all. He thought he was giving them a voice with his camera, but it never even aired." She sighed. "He's got such a sensitive soul, I know God can use him for mighty things if he only gives his life to the Lord."

"It sounds like God's already using him," Kennedy suggested, but Grandma Lucy wasn't listening.

"I pray every day for that boy to come back to Christ. And now he's off travelling around Asia. Same thing. Human rights abuses, refugee crises. Always ready to speak up for the downtrodden and oppressed. So he's off to China with his camera but without the Holy Spirit to guide him. I gave him a Bible, and I told him I'd be praying for him. You know, that's all any of us can do in these situations, right? What about that roommate of yours? Is she born again?"

Kennedy kept her voice low, glad that Willow was sufficiently distracted. "I don't think so."

Grandma Lucy stared over her spectacles. "I take it you've witnessed to her by now?"

Kennedy glanced at Willow, who was

snuggled up by Ray so they could share the same screen. "Well, I …"

"You can't ever be ashamed of the gospel," Grandma Lucy interrupted. "Your roommate … I can tell by the way she carries herself, that blue hair, those long earrings, that she's looking for something."

Kennedy wasn't sure you could discern that much about the state of a stranger's soul at first glance, but she didn't say anything. Something in Grandma Lucy's words had snuck past Kennedy's conversational barriers and found its mark in a conscience already ridden with guilt.

A year and a half sharing the same three-hundred square feet, and what had she done with that time? How many opportunities had she lost, opportunities to share the gospel with Willow, who was hurting, longing for more out of life whether or not her hair color had anything to do with her spiritual condition?

On the one hand, Kennedy was certain that if she were to bring up God or salvation, Willow would go off on one of her tirades against religion. So what was the point? Willow said once that Kennedy was the only

Christian she could stand to be around because she never tried to convert anyone. If Kennedy started preaching the gospel every minute of the day, telling Willow she was a sinner in danger of the fires of hell, that would only confirm her assumption that all Christians are judgmental jerks.

But even though her silence on the subject kept the peace between them, was that in Willow's best interest? Kennedy thought about the missionaries she'd been reading about in those biographies: Hudson Taylor, David Livingstone, Amy Carmichael. The Chinese called Gladys Aylward a foreign devil and threw mud at her the first day she stepped foot on foreign soil. But she had remained faithful to God's call and ended up leading hundreds to Christ.

Kennedy had never had mud thrown at her, had never been called horrid names, but maybe that was because she'd kept her faith so hidden. She thought about the refugees her parents trained to send back to North Korea as underground missionaries. How many of them would suffer imprisonment or death as a result of their witness? And here was Kennedy, scared of mentioning God because she didn't want to annoy her roommate.

Were her priorities that askew? Or was she just doing what God wanted her to do? What was it that Grandma Lucy had said earlier, something about nobody having to do more than God asked them to. Maybe Kennedy's job was to prove to Willow that not all Christians are out solely to win more converts or smugly judge sinful behavior. Maybe that's all God expected of her.

But how would Willow ever get saved if she never heard the gospel? Kennedy didn't like the guilt trip, Grandma Lucy's insinuation that if she really was a *born-again* believer she should have converted her roommate by now or else died trying like the martyrs of old.

Grandma Lucy laid her hand on Kennedy's forearm. "Now, you tell me your roommate's name, and I'm going to add her to my prayer list. Then I'll give you my phone number and you can let me know when she's been born again, all right?"

Kennedy sighed. "Her name's Willow."

Grandma Lucy pulled a tattered notebook out of her purse. "Willow," she repeated. "Oh, dear. She'll be one of the last ones, I'm afraid." She smiled and explained, "I keep my list alphabetized, so when I'm going to sleep I don't forget who's next on the list. I always start with my grand-daughter Alayna and make my way down from there. The good news is by the time I get to the Ws, I'll be nice and warmed up. If I haven't fallen asleep, that is."

Grandma Lucy's eyes twinkled, but Kennedy couldn't tell if she were making a joke or not. She didn't have time to wonder long before the bearded man in the turban jumped out of his chair with a startling shout.

"What's he think he's doing?" muttered the Seahawks fan with the BO. Several other passengers turned their heads as well.

The traveler pounded his fist into his seatback and yelled something frantic in Arabic.

The man in Carhartts stepped out of the bathroom and stood frozen in the aisle. An-other man lowered his head onto his tray table and covered it with his hands as if he were a first-grader in an earthquake drill.

The man in the turban yelled aggres-sively, waving his hands in the air as if to emphasize a point.

"Get down," a man hissed to Kennedy. "That maniac is about to take over the plane."

Ready for more Christian suspense that inspires your faith and keeps you turning pages WAY too late at night?

Dive into the Kennedy Stern series today!